H. C. ANDERSEN

THE EMPEROR'S NEW CLOTHES

AS RETOLD AND
ILLUSTRATED BY
S. T. MENDELSON

STEWART, TABORI & CHANG

NEW YORK

In memory of a brave truthsayer, Dimitri Dimitrievich Shostakovich
—S.T.M.

Copyright 1992 © S. T. Mendelson
Designed by Diana M. Jones
Jacket designed by Julie Rauer

Published in 1992 by
Stewart, Tabori & Chang
575 Broadway, New York, New York 10012

Library of Congress Cataloging-in-Publication Data
Mendelson, S. T.
   The emperor's new clothes / H.C. Andersen; retold and illustrated
by S.T. Mendelson.
      p. cm.
   Summary: A rascal sells a vain emperor an invisible suit of
clothes. Illustrated with animal characters.
   ISBN 1-55670-232-9
   [1. Fairy tales.] I. Andersen, H. C. (Hans Christian),
1805-1875. Kejserens nye klaeder. English. II. Title.
PZ8.M522Em 1992
[E]—dc20   91-42606
                                                  CIP

Distributed in the U.S. by
Workman Publishing, 708 Broadway
New York, New York 10003

Distributed in Canada by
Canadian Manda Group, P.O. Box 920 Station U
Toronto, Ontario, M8Z 5P9

Distributed in all other territories by
Little, Brown and Company, International Division
34 Beacon Street, Boston, Massachusetts 02108

Printed and bound by
Tien Wah Press (Pte), Ltd.,
Singapore
10 9 8 7 6 5 4 3 2 1

THE
EMPEROR'S
NEW
CLOTHES

Once upon a time there was an emperor who was much loved. Mostly by himself. After all, he was not just any emperor. He was the best dressed emperor the world had ever known. And even he himself was impressed by that.

Everyone told the emperor how magnificent he was, how rich he was, and how magnificently, richly dressed he was. The emperor quite agreed with them. He never for a moment suspected that everyone secretly thought he was quite silly and that his clothes showed it.

The truth of the matter is that there is no easy way to tell an emperor he has bad taste.

The emperor was, however, generous by nature (though mostly with himself), and used any excuse to create a holiday for his subjects. The highlight of every holiday

was the Grand Processional, during which all the emperor's subjects would loudly cheer the emperor and praise his latest imperial outfit as he rode through the streets.

Being as wise a ruler as he was beloved, the emperor had many spies in his empire—mostly in the garment district. He kept tabs on all the latest clothing trends, and time and again astounded everyone with the newest fashion before it even was a fashion.

It was from the reports of his many spies that the emperor came to learn of an incredible, magical tailor. Everyone agreed the tailor was incredible and magical, though no one could say exactly why. You see, no one had ever actually seen anything by way of a length of fabric or a stitch of thread from this tailor. Still, he had enough of a reputation to intrigue the emperor, who promptly sent for him.

"Well, my good fellow," the emperor said, "tell me what is so extraordinary about the clothing you make."

"Majesty, Your Highness, Emperor, Sir," replied the tailor, "the clothes I make are rich and rare and can only be seen by those of highest distinction. Through magic cunning, they are invisible to those who are unfit for their positions or who are unforgiveably silly—or both."

The emperor hired him on the spot.

"Make me an outfit of such clothing immediately," demanded the emperor. He thought to himself how splendid it would be to know which of his subjects were unfit or unforgiveably silly.

Only the best fabrics, threads, and especially jewels would do for such an incredible, magical tailor creating such a wondrous ensemble for an emperor with such exquisite taste. The emperor ordered the palace thrown open to

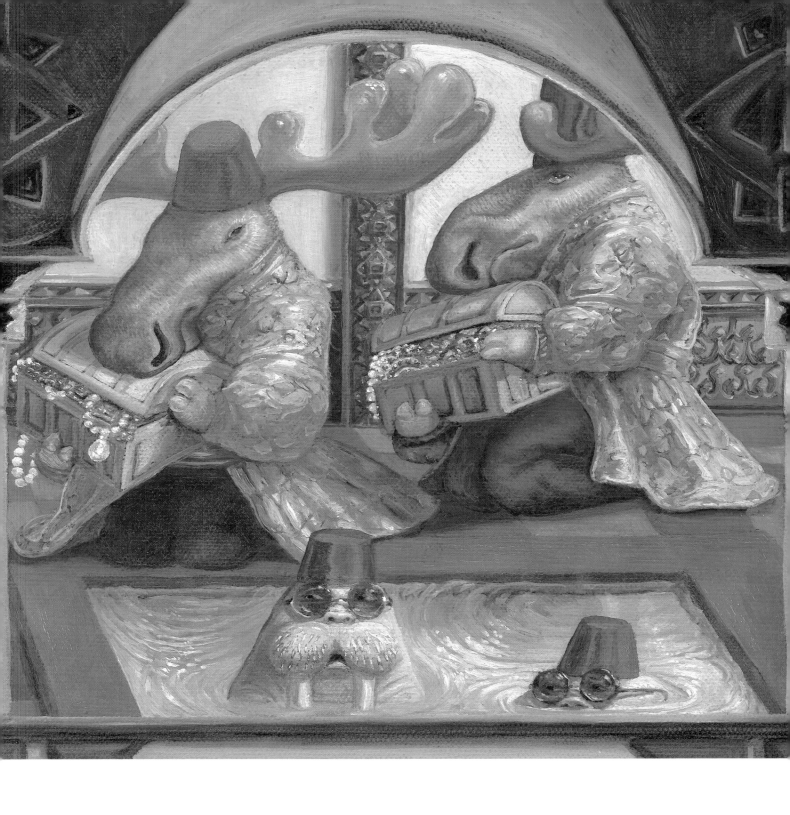

the tailor, including the treasury, which was quickly emptied by the tailor's many orders for gold and precious stones.

Daily, the emperor received reports on the progress of the robes from the tailor, who in all modesty proclaimed them to be the most beautiful in the universe. But these reports were not enough for the emperor.

The emperor had just enough dignity not to run through the halls of the palace himself for a peek at the tailor's work. Instead he sent his prime minister.

The prime minister was shocked. He saw nothing on the loom! Was he unfit to be prime minister? Surely he was just a little silly, not unforgiveably silly. This was simply too much. Not having an emperor's dignity, he ran all the way back to the emperor and made up a glowing account of the wondrous fabrics he had just been to see.

Thrilled with what he heard, but wanting to hear more, the emperor sent his lord admiral and captain of the guard to inspect the most beautiful clothing in the universe.

The lord admiral and the captain of the guard were shocked. Neither of them saw anything but the tailor busy at an empty loom! Could they be unfit for their positions? Surely they were no more silly than the average lord admiral and captain of the guard. This was simply too much. They ran all the way back to the emperor and delivered a report just as glowing as the prime minister's.

"An armada of cloth," said the lord admiral. "A phalanx of fashion," said the captain of the guard.

Even an emperor's dignity has limits. Unable to contain himself any longer, the emperor ran all the way through the palace to the tailor's rooms and burst in. The emperor was shocked. He saw nothing! It was preposterous to think he might be unfit or unforgiveably silly. After all, he was the emperor! This was really too much.

"The universe is surely too small a place for something as remarkably beautiful as this . . . as this . . . masterpiece!" declared the emperor. The tailor graciously accepted the imperial comment with a bow.

The emperor's cabinet met to discuss how best to celebrate the emperor's new clothes. After much bickering, debating, complimenting the emperor on his brilliance, and other all-around silliness, it was decided that nothing less than a Day of National Salvation would do.

Proclamations were sent throughout the empire, newspapers prepared to cover the grand event, the palace was repainted, and the streets were cleaned. Tension mounted as the great day approached.

The emperor, the prime minister, the lord admiral, and the captain of the guard were worried. What if it was discovered that they couldn't see the new clothes? Everyone would think them unfit for their positions or unforgiveably silly. What then?

At last the great day came.
The tailor took special care dressing the emperor, describing each article of clothing in great and glorious detail as he helped the emperor into it. Fortunately the tailor had the exclusive honor of assisting the emperor, for no one else would have been able to tell which garment was to go where and would surely hand the emperor his vest instead of his pants, or his shirt instead of his stockings.

The emperor preened himself to perfection.

Trumpets blared and drums rolled as the emperor in his full majesty left the gates of the palace. But from all the people gathered to cheer the emperor's new clothes, there arose only a shocked silence. They saw nothing. In that horrible

moment, before the crowds could collect their wits and loudly praise the emperor's magnificent—but invisible—robes, a child yelled out, "But, Mama, the emperor is wearing a girdle!"

All was lost. There was no doubt in the emperor's mind now. He had been . . . he was . . . wearing nothing. With a dignity only an emperor can muster, he held his head high, adjusted his girdle, turned around, and marched magnificently back into the palace.

All agreed that this retreat was the emperor's finest hour.